The Song
of a Bird

Charleen Mc Donald

Archway Publishing books may be ordered through booksellers or by contacting:

Archway Publishing
1663 Liberty Drive
Bloomington, IN 47403
www.archwaypublishing.com
844-669-3957

Because of the dynamic nature of the Internet, any web addresses or links contained in this book may have changed since publication and may no longer be valid. The views expressed in this work are solely those of the author and do not necessarily reflect the views of the publisher, and the publisher hereby disclaims any responsibility for them.

Any people depicted in stock imagery provided by Getty Images are models, and such images are being used for illustrative purposes only. Certain stock imagery © Getty Images.

ISBN: 978-1-6657-1761-8 (sc)
ISBN: 978-1-6657-1760-1 (e)

Print information available on the last page.

Archway Publishing rev. date: 03/03/2022

The Song of a Bird

By

Charleen Mc Donald

Illustrations by
Charleen Mc Donald

There was this little ole lady
who painted pictures on a card.
She painted birds and flowers
Sitting in her little back yard.

She painted red birds, yellow birds and birds of blue.

She painted black birds, brown birds,
and white ones too.

Spring time came,
and the sun warmed the land.

She worked diligently with her busy little hands.

She painted birds in the nest, up in a tree.
Sometimes there was a baby one,

And sometimes two or three.

She painted so many birds
She hung them on the wall by a string.
And suddenly, one day,
All the birds began to sing.

Their shrill little voices were so clear,
and so loud.
They sounded so happy as if singing on a cloud.

Sometimes their songs were very soft
and sometimes very low.
Sometimes they would sing so fast
and sometimes very slow.

When they were really excited
They would sing very high.
Their heads turned upward
As if singing to the sky!

The little ole lady would look at her
pictures every day
and perhaps talk to them in
some sort of way.

After spring time and summer,
the fall season was here.
This is the most beautiful season of the year.

All the leaves turned to red, gold, and brown.
So she painted birds in the tree tops
and birds on the ground.

Soon fall turned to winter
and one cold snowy day,
the little ole lady put her paints away.

There were so many thing she needed to do.
Cleaning, cooking, and some sewing too.

Each day she would dust the furniture
and sweep the floor.

But suddenly, one day,
the birds would sing no more.

The little ole lady now felt all alone.
She was just so lonesome
without the birds song.

So she picked up her phone
and thought she would make a call.
The birds seemed so sad,
they just hung on the wall.

Christmas time
was getting near
with snow flakes
covering the trees.
Raindrops dripping
from the roof
and icicles began
to freeze.

So the little ole lady got out her paints and
thought,
I'll just paint some Christmas cards.
They will be different from those I bought.

She began brushing
paints on a card.
A stream and a
frozen mist.

With every stroke of the brush she said,
There is nothing more beautiful than this.

She painted a little white church
with a bird on the steeple.
Snow covering the ground,
and the church full of people.

A few more strokes
of the brush,
The stars were
shining bright.
Suddenly the whole
world seemed to
become very quiet

From the windows the church lights glistened,
and everyone, everywhere, stood still to listen.

All across the lands
You could hear the church bells ring.

And in one great melody
all the birds began to sing.

The heavenly angels choir so beautifully joined in,
singing, "Glory to God, Good will among men."

What a wondrous sound,
every voice filled with love.
And the true spirit of Christmas
came down from above.

There is no sound more magical
that has ever been heard,
Than the voices of an angel choir,

and the Song of a Bird.

About the Author

Charleen McDonald

Charleen Mc Donald is a ninety-eight-year-old self taught writer, artist, and poet, in addition to being a mother, grandmother, minister, and friend to all who know her.

Printed in the United States
by Baker & Taylor Publisher Services